One Spring at Tilladrum

HOLLY WYLD

For my two sunbeams,
with all my love x

Chapter One

"Rehab?"

Wren Collett's tea went down the wrong way, and it was necessary to splutter and cough for a bit before she could progress her line of questioning any further.

"Did you just say *rehab*, Dad?"

Her father flushed. He was somewhat prone to mangling his words and Wren sensed — or at least *hoped* — that's what was going on here.

"Rehab. Yes," he said, blinking innocently. "Well, I mean, *no*. But also, *yes*..."

Colin Collett frowned and poured a little more tea into his daughter's mug. "Sort of thing..."

"Rehab, Dad? Rehab. *Me?*" Wren took a gulp of her topped-up tea. "That's just... Surely you remember the *one* time I tried–" she dropped her voice to a whisper, "*–weed?*" before carrying on in a normal volume, "*Dad? That one* time? When I was seventeen? Surely you remember? It didn't go well. You held my hair..."

Her father grimaced at the memory. Then his face softened, and he reached a hand across the table and squeezed one of hers. "Of *course* I remember. I also remember banning you from attending that party."

"I know. Sorry about that. I was in my rebellious phase. Anyway, the point being, I was a lightweight then and, guess what? I'm *still* a lightweight!

1

I mean, for goodness' sake! You'd *think*, wouldn't you, that at this point I'd be *all over* the gins-and-tonics and the glasses of wine and the tubs of ice cream and the... the... *Percy Pigs*... wouldn't you?"

She did love *Percy Pigs*.

"You'd *think*, wouldn't you," she went on, "that given the *circumstances*, I'd be all over *anything* that could take the edge off – if not obliterate completely – the brutal memory, the total and utter emotional *carnage*, Dad, of being JILTED AT THE ALTAR! Wouldn't you? *Wouldn't* you?"

Colin Collett squeezed his daughter's hand even tighter.

"All right, all right. Don't get in a tizz."

A tizz. The apocalypse could be raining down upon them and her dad would still gently caution her not to get in a *tizz*.

"I'm not in a *tizz*, Dad!"

She *was* becoming quite exasperated, though.

"I'm *annoyed* at myself! I'm annoyed at my hopeless inability to drown my sorrows at the one moment in my life when they really need drowning! I'm *annoyed* about this weird, late-flowering streak of pure *masochism* that makes me unable to face even a single cheerful glass of red wine right now. Or a square of chocolate. Or a flipping *Percy Pig!* And I *love* Percy Pigs!"

Colin Collett had both of his daughter's hands in his now.

"Yes. Yes, I know. I know..." he said, squeezing her hands reassuringly.

He gave it a moment, allowing the dust to settle.

"Rant over?"

Wren managed a half smile and nodded. "Yes," she said quietly. "Rant over. I'm just saying that you can probably remove rehab from your list of Things That Might Fix Wren."

Her father gave her hands one last encouraging squeeze, then released them and topped up his own mug of tea. "You know very well there's no such list," he said pointedly, setting down the teapot, and generating a sound in his throat that was closing in on a *harrumph*. "You, Wren, are not someone in need of fixing. Don't let anyone tell you otherwise."

Wren stared down at her tea. She didn't want him to see that she had tears in her eyes. Didn't want him to know that someone *had* told her otherwise. In no uncertain terms. The someone in question being the man she'd thought she was marrying – on the day he'd been *supposed* to be marrying her.

For the millionth time, she pushed the memories of that day away.

"That *said*, however…" her father was venturing on, prompting Wren to look up and catch his nervous little eyebrow waggle, his nervous bit of finger drumming.

Here we go.

"That *said*… I *do* think a rehab of *sorts* would do you good."

Gah. Wren plunged her head into her hands. *Back to square one.*

"Sorry, Dad. I'm really not following," she said, closing her eyes. She was starting to get a headache.

Colin Collett needlessly rearranged the tea things laid out between them in the centre of their kitchen table.

"I don't mean in the way of a *clinic* or anything," he said tentatively. "You know, for drugs and alcohol and what have you. I don't mean *that*. I just mean, well, a break, I suppose. A change of scene. Some time away. Somewhere *nice*."

Despite the band of pain that was beginning to tighten around her skull, Wren doubled down on her efforts to get onto her dad's wavelength.

A thought occurred. A little bit of sense – a little bit of *light* pushing through the clouds.

"But rehab Dad? Are you sure you don't mean… *retreat*?"

Her father's eyes lit up. He straightened in his chair and started pointing at Wren and waggling his finger like he did when they played *charades* and she'd just guessed the answer.

"Yes!" he said, sending tea sloshing over the top of his mug. "That's it! That's the thing, Wren! A *retreat*. A *retreat* is what I'm getting at!"

Wren studied his face carefully while making a distracted effort to mop up the spilt tea.

"Okaaay…" she said slowly, narrowing her eyes, feeling her way – because the jury was still out on what *exactly* her father was getting at, here.

But Colin Collett, emboldened by his daughter's *okaaay*, was already reaching for his shirt pocket.

Wren angled her head and narrowed her eyes further. Her father had an expression on his face that she knew very well. An expression, entirely unique to him, of pure mischief mingled with a dollop of pride.

What was he up to?

She watched him retrieve, and then unfold, the contents of his shirt pocket. It was a small printed flyer, which he proceeded to hold up in front of her for inspection, his eyes all big and bright and hopeful.

3

"Well?" he said. "What d'you think?"

In large-ish letters at the top, Wren saw the words *Tilladrum Estate*. She frowned. What, exactly, and where, exactly, was *Tilladrum Estate*? Gently, she took the flyer from him and began to read on.

TILLADRUM ESTATE

Help Needed:

For Walled Garden Restoration Project

Tilladrum Estate, Primrose Island, Outer Hebrides

All and any experience appreciated. Enthusiasm a must!

-Accommodation
-Use of car
-Weekly stipend

Enquiries welcome.
Please contact: Freya Struthers

There were lots of little tear-off strips at the bottom with her phone number on them.

Wren continued to study the flyer for a moment.

A walled garden restoration project.

On a *Scottish* island.

In the *Outer Hebrides*.

"Dad," she said, lifting her gaze to meet her father's eyes. "What are you up to?"

Colin Collett cleared his throat. "Yes, well, see, it's not so much what I'm *up* to, exactly, Wren," he said. "It's more a case of what I've, er, *done*..."

Chapter Two

"But a *walled garden*, Dad? Me? *Me* look after a walled garden? *Restore* a walled garden?"

The expression on Wren's face at this point could best be described as *highly dubious.*

"The first – but definitely not the last – problem with this idea, Dad, is... I don't know the first thing about walled gardens!"

Colin Collett was having none of it.

"Oh come on," he said. "What about all those episodes of *Gardener's World* you watched during lockdown? And the small fortune you spend every month on gardening magazines! More visits than I care to count to Oxfam and the Red Cross, buying up all those old gardening books. And that's before we even get to all the time you spend pottering about on that balcony of yours..."

"Yes, Dad," Wren shot back. "Balcony. *Balcony.* Geraniums. Basil. There may have been daffodils at some point. And *pottering*, Dad. *Pottering* being the operative word..."

Wren's father batted away her protests.

"It says here..." he tapped the flyer, "...all and *any* experience. They're looking for enthusiasm, mostly. And you've plenty of that."

"I know you mean well, Dad, and I love the idea of disappearing to some lovely secret garden in the Hebrides... The *Outer* Hebrides..."

Wren's voice hitched in her throat just then, and her protest trailed off.

Because she *did* love the idea, and for some reason, saying it out loud made her want to cry. It was quite possible that disappearing off to a secret garden in the Hebrides... *Outer* Hebrides... was the very thing her soul, and her trampled – if not completely broken – heart was crying out for right now.

Of course, her dad, being her dad, knew that.

She tried to pick up where she'd left off. An auto-pilot protest – albeit a thin one. "But, I mean, I can't just take off, can I? I couldn't just–"

Colin Collett leaned closer, and once again took her hands.

"Why not? Why couldn't you?"

Wren stared at him. In addition to her situation with Si–

–with her now-vanished husband-to-be, she was also four months into the unpaid sabbatical she'd arranged with work.

The truth was, she wasn't well supplied with reasons *not* to just take off.

For the umpteenth time that morning, another searing flashback of her abject humiliation elbowed its way to the front of her consciousness.

Her. Alone at the altar of St Ninian's. Heat rising into her cheeks – and staying there. Hushed gossipy murmurs starting up and rippling their way through the congregation.

She'd wanted the ground to swallow her whole.

But above all, she'd wanted to know why Simon had stopped loving her.

She closed her eyes, and with intense determination pushed all of it aside. Instead, she pulled a whole raft of *different* imagery from the recesses of her mind.

Roses tangling and scrambling over walls.

Ancient apple trees arching prettily in neat espalier arrangements.

Colour-bursts of hollyhocks and great drifts of wild fennel.

Little potager squares of mint and thyme and rosemary and–

–He was right. Her father was right. Why not? *Why couldn't she?*

She opened her eyes again.

On her father's face – a pinkish flush. And a small, mysterious smile.

"Have you done something, Dad?" she said, the tiniest spark of something new and hopeful lighting in her chest. "Have you *done* something?"

Wren's father swallowed.

"Don't be mad," he said. "But... yes. Yes, I've gone a bit rogue."

* * *

Indeed, he had.

It took a second pot of tea, and a lengthy *q and a* session besides, but Wren's quizzing of her father soon enough revealed that Colin Collett had taken it upon himself to call Freya Struthers at Tilladrum Estate to convince her that his daughter would be very well suited to the task of restoring the old walled garden there.

"Dad!"

Wren was impressed by his chutzpah. Like her, he was actually quite shy. But then again, how many times had he told her he'd do anything for her?

Her heart squeezed. *She'd never doubted that.*

"Go on," she urged. "What did you say?" She was peering at him over her mug and taking small nervous sips of the fresh tea.

He smiled sheepishly. *Proudly.* "I told her you were a plants nut."

Wren grinned. *This was true.*

"A plants nut that had ended up selling car insurance for a living."

Er, yeah. This was also true...

And Wren had never exactly figured out how that had happened. Certainly, her dad was also baffled by it.

"And?"

"I told her that while you hadn't been able to try your skills much beyond a small balcony that overlooks a parade of shops on the outskirts of Reading, your knowledge of plants, and your genuine enthusiasm for anything to do with gardening, meant that she wouldn't regret hiring you. *Enthusiasm*, see? Like it says on the flyer?"

"Okay. Good. That's really good." Wren was warming to all this, now. "Anything else?"

"Yes. I told her that you'd recently suffered a personal setback."

Wait, what?

"A personal setback? Dad. Tell me you didn't go into the whole being jilted thing."

Colin Collett cleared his throat.

"Well, I did."

"Dad! No!"

"It's relevant to your application, Wren!" he protested. "Insofar as it's relevant to your state of mind!"

"But Dad it's private! I don't want every—"

"And Wren," he said, interrupting gently, "the same thing happened to her."

"Wh— what?"

Colin Collett nodded. "This Freya lady. Freya Struthers? The same thing happened to her. She was stood up. Jilted. Left standing like a lemon at the altar. Just like you. And quite a few members of the press there, too, in her case. *Paparazzi*."

"Really?" Wren began to tear up. "The press? Poor thing," she murmured. "Poor thing."

Her father nodded again. "Five years ago it was, I think she said."

Wren pulled a tissue from her cardigan and blew her nose.

Five years... Wren was only at four months.

"And Wren..." her dad picked up again, "D'you know what else she said?"

Wren sniffed and swiped a few remaining tears away. "What?"

"Two things. The first thing was, 'tell your daughter she's going to be okay.'"

He may as well have taken a pin to a balloon.

Wren burst into tears on hearing those words, and her father – tears in his own eyes now, too – rounded the table and pulled her up and into a hug.

"You're going to be okay, Wren," he said gently. "I say so. And Freya Struthers says so too. Okay?"

Wren laughed a little. "Okay..." she managed. And then when back to crying. Because crying was all she could do in that moment.

"And Wren?" said her father, taking her messy tear-streaked face into his hands, "Mmhmm?" she sniffled.

"The second thing Freya Struthers said?"

"Mmhhuh?"

"She said, 'Tell your daughter to pack her bags. Because she's coming to Tilladrum.'"

Chapter Three

Freya and Jasper Struthers had been arranging and rearranging the furniture in the living room of Gardener's Cottage for the past hour and forty-five minutes, with Freya, in particular, deeply absorbed in the detail of it all.

"...and the evenings are still quite cold, really," she was murmuring – mostly to herself, "so I think we want the most comfortable chair – squishy plum velvet? – to be the closest one to the wood burner, meaning the old wingback could go–"

"–Freya," said her brother.

"–over there. Beside the–"

"Freya," Jasper said again, and then more emphatically, "Frey."

Freya looked up, Jasper's interruption finally having the desired effect.

"Sorry, what?"

"Seamus, Freya." Jasper nodded at the tall brooding figure standing in the doorway of the living room. "Seamus is here."

Freya blinked, looked over to the doorway, and saw that sure enough, Seamus, Tilladrum's woodsman, was standing there, waiting politely for her to acknowledge him.

"Seamus!" Freya said. "I'm so sorry! And also, good morning!"

The woodsman smiled.

"Morning, Ms Struthers," he said.

Freya shook her head and put her hands on her hips.

"Honestly. I'm actually going to conk you over the head if you don't drop the *Ms Struthers* thing," she said. "We're not in the nineteenth century. I'm not into the whole cap-doffing thing."

Jasper and Seamus both laughed. And Freya laughed, too, adding, "Please, Seamus. You have to stop."

Seamus quirked a smile. "Fair enough. Anyway, I've a decent load of quartered firewood out there in the trailer, *Freya*. Want me to stack it in the shed?"

Freya smiled. "That'd be brilliant. And..." she reached for the basket that was sitting beside the wood burner, "...could I grab a basketful off you for in here, too?"

Seamus nodded and went back outside leaving Freya a moment to dart an admonishing look at her brother.

"How long was I prattling on for while he was stood waiting? You should have bopped me over the head or something!"

Jasper offered her a shrug and a smile. "A while. But I wouldn't worry about it," he chuckled. "I don't think he minded."

People tended *not* to mind when it came to Freya. It was next to impossible to be mad at her. She was bottled sunshine. Bottled goodness. Even as a child, she'd been unfailingly kind to everyone. Particularly – Jasper had to admit – her *at times* rather mean-spirited younger brother.

Hopefully, he was making it up to her now. Five years ago, Freya had in the space of three days lost a fiancé and gained – along with Jasper – a crumbling country estate on the island.

And since that time, he had done what he could to at least share, if not whenever he could *carry*, the bulk of the worry – and the lion's share of the financial burden.

In any case, five years on from their uncle's inheritance, they had settled into a routine of sorts. A routine largely concerned with doing anything and everything they could think of to keep Tilladrum House, and Tilladrum Estate, ticking over financially.

Weddings and location shoots were the backbone of their income now.

And though they were both aware of their privilege in calling Tilladrum home, and calling themselves its custodians, it was a privilege that came with its fair share of sleepless nights.

Even so, selfless Freya was forever telling Jasper to *go*.

Get out there! she'd say. *See the world! Wander the earth. I did. So should you...*

She worried about him, he knew.

"D'you ever think we might be staring down the barrel of a bit of a weird, early and possibly quite cc-dependent middle age, Jas?" she'd muse – or words to that effect – from time to time.

And he'd laugh and usually answer "Yes. All the time..." – or words to *that* effect.

But it pained him to think that in addition to all the other things she worried about, Freya really did worry about *him*, and about the possibility he might feel stuck. Stuck with her and stuck at Tilladrum and just, well, *stuck* in general.

Which, fine, to some extent was true. The *stuck in general* part in any case.

All the same, Jasper usually encouraged Freya to drop the subject whenever she picked up again with one of her go-and-see-the-world speeches – even if privately he was willing to concede she had a point. They *were* both staring down the barrel of middle age.

Freya was forty. He was thirty-eight.

Perhaps he really should leave the island. Perhaps he should–

But no. It was... *complicated*. And not merely because of his sense of sibling duty to Freya. Or his taking seriously his custodianship of Tilladrum.

It was complicated because, well, because of Lara. And the tentative – if ever-increasingly daft – hope that one day, she might come back.

Jasper sighed and moved to the window in hopes of switching his thoughts onto other matters.

Such as the walled garden. And the imminent arrival of one Wren Collett.

He was quite pleased about it all, actually. It had been his idea to overhaul the garden. Well, more realistically, given their budget – or lack thereof – to find an enthusiastic volunteer to kickstart the process.

He'd unearthed a huge archive of ledgers and notebooks and drawings and planting schemes in Tilladrum's library. And he had immediately been struck by the idea that it would be a very great pity not to do something with them. With *it*.

And Freya had agreed, seeing at once the walled garden's potential, once restored, to be folded into Tilladrum's wedding and photo shoot offerings.

So here they were, readying Gardener's Cottage for Wren – a wounded bird, by all accounts, to put with the heartbroken Seamus.

Freya had a radar for such things. Wounds. And heartbreak.

Little wonder, really, since she'd weathered plenty of both herself.

Might Freya be looking for the stars to align for this young gardener and their Dubliner woodsman? Possibly. Although the poor guy was still quite evidently mourning his late wife.

Jasper would leave all of that to Freya.

As for himself – he was not inclined to waste any more time on the potential alignment of stars. His star – and that of the woman his heart had never properly recovered from loving – were about as far flung out of alignment as it was possible to be.

They always had been.

He turned away from the window, and away from the garden.

"Frey?" he called. "What do you want me to do with this coffee table?"

Chapter Four

Getting from Reading to the Outer Hebrides had been no mean feat.

Wren found herself mentally chalking up the various stages of the journey that had just now culminated in an impromptu lift from Tam, the island postman – or *postie*, as he'd explained – and on the point of taking the Tam-advised shortcut through some woodland to Tilladrum – or *the big house*, as Tam had also explained.

Lift from Dad. Train from Reading to London. Tube to Heathrow. Flight to Glasgow. Flight to the island – and oh, that landing – on the beach! That tiny plane – landing on the beach! And then, yes, a very chatty lift all the way around the island to the edge of the Tilladrum estate, courtesy of Tam-the-postie.

Wren began stepping carefully through the swathe of bluebells that carpeted the woodland ahead of her.

She breathed in deeply. The air smelled green and new, like rain.

She went further into the woods, the ground beneath soft with moss and damp pinecones.

Birch and rowan.

Scots pine and juniper.

She was walking through a remnant of old Caledonian forest. It felt magical. *Other-worldly.*

Sweet spring scents and cool air. Chirping birds and soft breezes stirring the leaves... It was the loveliest kind of sensory overload, in fact, it was the loveliest–

"Oh my goodness," Wren murmured, stopping her thoughts in their tracks. And stopping her *feet* in *their* tracks.

Because she had arrived in a clearing that perfectly framed Tilladrum House. She recognised it immediately from the sketch on the flyer.

It sat proudly on a gentle rise in the land, gently aglow in the low afternoon light. And Wren could also make out, a little distance behind it, the tall brick-and-lime ivy-straggled walls of Tilladrum's walled garden.

She smiled and took a breath – and wasn't at all surprised a moment later to find her eyes welling with tears.

She was *here*.

Chapter Five

Locating Gardener's Cottage had been easy. It was literally built into the walls of the walled garden.

By arrangement, Freya had left the old iron key to the cottage – burglars not a thing around here it would seem – in a nook beside the door, along with a note.

Dear Wren,

Firstly, welcome!

Secondly, I am SO sorry neither I nor my brother could be here to welcome you in person. We'll be back from the mainland tomorrow morning.

In the meantime, I hope hope hope you'll find what you need inside.

Can't wait to meet you!!

F x

Wren smiled. Freya had a way of making her feel like she was an old friend.

She creaked open the front door and hooked her coat and bag onto wall pegs just inside it.

Then she proceeded through to the kitchen.

Where her heart lifted. And stayed lifted.

It was *beautiful*.

"Oh my goodness," Wren found herself murmuring again. "It's so lovely..."

She'd expected – would have been happy with – something basic and serviceable as far as the free accommodation aspect went. A few sticks of second-hand furniture. A few basic bits of crockery and cooking equipment.

But *this* was not *that*.

She felt like pinching herself. Felt like she had strayed onto a photo shoot for *Country Living*.

The loving touches. The care and attention to detail.

Again... *Freya*.

Wren still hadn't met her, but somehow this woman – from five hundred miles away – had reached out a hand to her and made her feel, well, better. Had made her feel like she could come back from *it*. The jilting.

No, that she *would* come back from it.

The walls of the kitchen were a pale mustard yellow, perfectly setting off the cheerful blues of the jumbled Wedgwood plate collection housed in the dresser that faced the window.

In the middle of the room, there was a long refectory table covered in a vintage paisley tablecloth, and behind that was an old Rayburn, polished to a high gleam, and snuggled deep in the chimney recess, radiating its mellow warmth into the kitchen and the rooms beyond.

Wren continued through to the living room to find a large squishy sofa, two deep armchairs angled towards the wood burner – and two sweet, smaller chairs snuggled in the window bay.

All the soft furnishings and curtains were in happily clashing florals and velvets and tartans. It made Wren smile to look at them.

And vases – little glass and porcelain and painted vases everywhere – all stuffed with cyclamen and bluebells and snowdrops.

Wren swiped away another tear. Was it possible to feel that you were *home* in a place in which you'd never previously set foot?

It must be, she concluded. Because she did.

* * *

If walking the rooms of the cottage had made Wren a little emotional, stepping out into the walled garden surfaced something else entirely.

A heady mix of wonder and awe laced with... *a sizeable squidge of alarm.*

Wren swallowed.

The walled garden was, she now saw as she hurriedly stepped into her overalls – absolutely *huge*.

"Two acres?" she murmured. "This has to be at least two acres..."

Utterly tangled. Completely overgrown. And yes, vast.

But it was a dream. It was a *dream*.

She began to walk, scanning, noting and assessing as she went. The whole space was more or less a square that had been subdivided into four smaller squares and laid with slightly domed brick pathways – one main path going around the perimeter, others crisscrossing the interior.

Wren stopped for a moment so that she could turn a slow, full circle, wanting to take it in all at once.

She had no difficulty seeing past the tangles and knee-high – okay, in places, *waist-high* – wilderness that currently prevailed.

She could *exactly* picture what it once had been.

And she could *exactly* picture what it could be again.

And it occurred to her, not for the first time since deep-diving into her research, that a walled garden could be every bit as beautiful as it was functional.

She'd done a ton of reading in the days before her departure, and during her multi-stage journey to the island. And everything she had absorbed from her books now made much more sense in this physical, tangible form.

She turned north and south, east and west, figuring out the various elevations. She took in the towering walls – sixteen or eighteen feet, easily, she guessed – of brick and lime-mortar construction. Just what was needed to retain the heat and protect everything inside them from wind and frost.

And she took in again the lovely Gardener's Cottage which, as she'd already discovered, had been built into one of the walls.

A thirty-second commute, she smiled to herself. And how very much lovelier than her daily schleps across Reading to her cubicle-bound desk job in the insurance offices.

On the wall opposite the cottage – and straight out of *The Secret Garden*

– was a heavily weathered timber door. It was just about still openable, Wren discovered on wandering over to try it, despite its iron hardware having rusted over.

She continued her recce around the perimeter of the garden and found various additional outbuildings both inside and outside the walls for potting and storage and cold framing.

And she ended her exploration at the northernmost wall where the wooden-shuttered Victorian glasshouse still stood, and where the gardeners of the day would no doubt have tended oranges and peaches and pineapples.

Amazing. The tables at Tilladrum must have groaned under the weight of it all.

But yes… The gardeners of the day. *Gardeners.* Plural.

Still, that was then and this was now. Wren knew that Freya and her brother had to scrape every penny together each month just to break even. So there was no team. Just her. Well, her, with some occasional help from the Tilladrum woodsman should she need it, according to Freya.

Seamus, was it? A man of few words, by all accounts.

A small shiver went through her.

This was going to be a huge task, no doubt about it.

And it was also going to be *by far* the most exciting thing she'd ever had the chance to be involved in.

Could she do this? Could she pull it off?

She plucked Herbert bear from one of the deep front pockets of her twill boiler suit.

Herbert had been her dad's bear when he was a boy. And then he'd been hers.

Still was.

He was matted and worn. He'd sustained a sub-standard repair job to the velvet patch on his left paw. His once-smart bow was faded and frayed, and his once-bright glass eyes were now scratched and dull.

He was perfect.

"What d'you think Herbs?" Wren said, balancing him on top of a lovely old verdigris sundial so that she could get a picture of her co-adventurer in the walled garden and send it to her dad.

"Think I can pull this off?"

There was a pause.

"Of course you can, ma'am," said Herbert – by way of Wren's mouth. "Not a doubt in my mind."

"Yeah," Wren said, grinning and looking around once more. "Yeah. I agree," she said, snapping a few photos of the beloved family mascot.

"Dad," she began, "...oh, forgive me, Herbert, *Colonel Collett* has requested regular field reports from you. So don't let him down, okay?"

"I wouldn't dream of it, ma'am," Herbert bear said – again by way of Wren's mouth.

Wren nodded her approval. He was a very proper bear. Very precise, and, well, quite A-type – Wren and her father having cooked up between them something of a Captain-Mainwaring-from-Dad's-Army persona for him over the years.

"Colonel Collett shall have a full report by eighteen hundred hours, ma'am," said Herbert.

"Good stuff, Herbs," said Wren, snapping a few final photos of him to send to her dad later. "Good stuff."

She closed her eyes for a moment and took a long, deep breath.

She was far away from the memory of her so-called wedding day.

She was far away from all thoughts of Si– *The Jilter*.

She was far away, in fact, from *everything*.

And it was wonderful.

She exhaled and smiled and opened her eyes.

Just in time to see a wily crow swoop down and grab Herbert bear off the sundial.

It was slow-motion horror. The sight – burning itself onto her retinas – of her childhood teddy bear being carried off into the sky in a thuggish and violent flapping of black-feathered wings.

"No!" she yelled. "Herbert! Nooooo....!"

Wren gave chase immediately – alternately running and stomping and scanning the sky and the woods beyond for signs of the feathered thief.

"I'm coming Herbs!" she yelled. "I'm coming!"

Herbert bear was *not* about to become nesting material for a crow!

Not on *HER* watch!

Chapter Six

Seamus O'Neil, the woodsman at Tilladrum, was frowning.

Frowning and watching.

Watching and frowning.

But mostly frowning.

A woman in overalls was stomping his way, and yelling angrily. About herbs.

Seamus frowned some more, and shoved his hands in his pockets.

What was *that* about?

Wait.

A thought.

Not... *Surely not?* She wasn't the *gardener*, was she?

What was her name? *Wendy*? Stomping about all deranged-like. Shouting her head off about herbs and giving out about *crows?*

Seamus groaned inwardly. And then also outwardly for good measure.

The boiler suit.

The wellies.

The general timing. Today *was* the arrival day for the gardener, if he wasn't mistaken.

So this nut... This was the gardener?

Seamus was assailed by a deeply, deeply sinking feeling that it was.

Glum-faced and resigned, he continued to monitor her approach.

Until, that is, his attention was snagged by a soft *thud* behind him.

He turned around.

Huh.

A scruffy thing. An old teddy bear. Apparently having just dropped out of the sky.

"Bit random," Seamus mumbled, eyeing the thing with a raised brow.

He wandered over to it and picked it up.

"You okay, Mr Ted?" he said.

The bear seemed the stoic type. The stiff-upper-lip sort.

Seamus nodded. "Good." Then tucked the bear under his arm.

Wait a minute...

Several dots began to connect in Seamus's head. Per this bear. And per the strident *loon* marching up the hill.

He placed the bear on a nearby tree stump. Just in case.

And sure enough, right on cue, here she was.

The strident loon.

The nut.

The gardener.

Wendy.

She came stomping into the clearing. "Herbert!" she was calling. "Herbs! Where are you?"

Seamus stayed where he was – arms folded. Assessment mode activated.

Oh yeah. She was clearly another one of Freya's little projects. You could tell. To a man. To a woman. They all somehow embodied something of the sad and the lost.

And he should know. Being that he was one of them.

He shook his head. He could do without it, to be fair. The company. The inevitable questions. Inevitable co-worker-y, colleague-y, let's-be-pals stuff.

He could do without *all that* completely – and he could do without this *Wendy* altogether.

"Herbert! Herbs! Where are you?" the woman called again. She hadn't noticed Seamus.

Seamus blew out his cheeks, glanced behind him at the stoic, if raggedy-looking bear and said with a raised eyebrow, "Herbert, I presume?"

* * *

Wren had been scanning. Like a Terminator – sent from the future – scanning the tree tops for anything remotely *crow*. And scanning the forest floor for anything remotely *bear*.

She'd stomped all the way back to the old woods on seeing Herbert's feathered abductor flap in that general direction with Herbert in its clutches, and now she'd reached the top of the hill she stood under the tree canopy, hands on her hips, swivelling her head this way and that, trying again to locate Herbert's kidnapper.

"I'm telling you," she was yelling at the tree tops, "...if you remove even one, one *wisp* of that bear's stuffing – I *promise* you. I will *not* be held responsible for my–"

"Can I help you?"

Wren's not-quite-fully-thought-through crow threat was interrupted by a manly, Irish-accented voice.

She whirled around.

A very tall, broad, swarthy-looking guy was standing a few feet away from her.

He raised an eyebrow at her. "Can I help you?" he said again. Flatly.

"Oh. Um. Hi. Hello," Wren said cautiously, and with a frown for good measure.

The man didn't reciprocate with any further offerings. So Wren was forced to.

"Yeah. Hi. Sorry. But I'm... I'm dealing with a situation here."

The man raised his other eyebrow now, and also tipped up his chin a bit. Wren took this as a sort of wordless, manly, listening kind of gesture.

"Situation?" he said.

"Yes," she said, clearing her throat. And also cringing a bit inside. "A situation."

Possibly the man's mouth quirked a bit in amusement. It was hard to tell, given his otherwise utterly stony expression.

"You see, my um, my, my... bear... that is, my *teddy*," she cleared her throat again, deeply regretting having started down this conversational road, "...my teddy bear was... taken just now."

"I see."

His mouth definitely did quirk. He was definitely laughing at her. Discreetly. But still laughing at her.

And could she blame him? No. No, she could not.

22

Taken? A taken bear? What was this? A Liam Neeson movie?

"Taken?" said the man.

Perhaps he was wondering the same.

"Yes. Taken."

"Taken, as in stolen?"

"I mean... effectively, yes. Well, kidnapped. Bearnapped, let's say."

The Irishman's mouth quirked again.

Wren actually didn't care. She went back to scanning the trees, scanning the forest floor. She was feeling increasingly bereft about Herbert bear's fate.

And perhaps the swarthy-looking guy sensed this. Because he seemed to be easing up a bit on the trying-not-to-laugh thing.

There might even have been a softening of his expression from stony to *slightly less stony.*

He furrowed his brow and shifted from one foot to the other. "So, I mean it could be coincidence like," he said. "But... I've just been talking to a bear. A teddy bear, that is."

Wren brightened.

"What? You have?"

The man nodded. "Little fella? About so big?" He made a brief measuring gesture with his hands.

"Yes. Yes – a bear. About that big, yes. Do you—"

Splodge

Splodge

Splodge splodge sploage

Rain started to patter all around them, spattering off the foliage – and instantaneously drenching Wren and the Irishman.

Not that he seemed to notice.

He tilted his head. Indicated over his shoulder.

"Over there," he said, indicating a tree stump a few feet away.

"The little guy was over there last time I saw him."

Wren followed the man's cue. Sure enough, there he was – *Herbert* – safe and sound on a tree stump.

"Herbs!" Wren darted over to him and scooped him up and gave him a hug because she was way, way past any embarrassment by now and just very, very happy to see that Herbert hadn't been disembowelled and relieved of his eyes.

No. He was the same old Herbs. Apart from one thing. Wren noticed it straight away. He *smelled* different. *Faint trace of woodsmoke. And the faintest trace of a heathery sort of soap.*

She inhaled him for a moment, and by the time she thought of turning around to thank the guy, the guy had hefted a sizeable length of timber onto his shoulder and was backing away from her.

"See you, Wendy," he was saying. "You *are* Wendy, I take it? The gardener?"

Wendy?

"No. Well – yes, but—"

"Okay, well, I'd appreciate it if you'd... stay out of my way, basically, Wendy," he said in a flat tone as he backed away from her. "I'm not one for company."

Of course. Wren was rapidly catching up. This Irish guy – he was the woodsman. Seamus.

Wren opened her mouth to speak.

"Well, I don't – I mean, shouldn't we... try to..."

But her protest trailed off when it occurred to her that she wasn't exactly sure what she wanted to say.

Not that *Seamus* was listening. He was halfway down the hill already.

"Yeah. No offence, like, Wendy," he called over his shoulder. "But if you could keep out of my way..."

Wren watched him go, her mouth falling open a little further.

"...I'd appreciate it."

Wren made a face.

"Wren!" she called after him.

"My name is *Wren!*"

Chapter Seven

Rude, frankly. Just very, very rude.

Wren had passed an afternoon, an evening and various segments of the *night* revisiting Seamus-the-woodman's rudeness.

And now she was revisiting it again. In the middle of the morning. As she strode towards the impressive front door of Tilladrum house.

She tutted and shook her head as if to clear out the incumbent thoughts.

Look at this, she told herself instead, craning her neck and doing her best to absorb and appreciate the house's beautiful architecture, and the lovely view down to the coast afforded by its elevated position.

But...

Keep out of his way?

Keep out of his way?

And...

Not one for company?

What made him think *she* was?

Okay. Okay, so *possibly* she'd come over as... kind of pathetic. What with her whole teddy bear drama and everything.

But still. She resented the presumption!

"Tell you what, Mr Seamus. Mr Woodsman," she muttered, crunching emphatically over the gravel towards the house, passing as she did so a pair of strutting resplendent peacocks. "I'll be quite happy to stay out of your way… Quite, *quite* happy!"

"Wren? Is that you?"

A female voice behind her.

Wren stopped in her tracks and turned around in time to see a beaming, kind-faced woman striding towards her. She knew straight away it was Freya.

Instinctively, like they were the oldest friends, the two women skipped the handshakes and went straight into a hug.

"I'm so glad you made it," said Freya. "It's a long way to come."

"I'm so glad too," said Wren "and I can't wait to get stuck in. Oh and Freya, the cottage? It's just lovely. Thank you."

"Oh, d'you like it?" Freya's smile widened. "I'm so glad. I wanted it to be nice for you."

"It's so much more than nice. It's… I can see how much care you put into getting it ready for me."

"Oh, but we're bringing you such a long way from home and paying you pennies. So, please, the pleasure – and the thanks – are all mine."

They smiled at each other.

"Come on," said Freya. "Let's grab a coffee. I've got a ton of stuff in the library for you."

The peacocks went rustling and preening ahead of them. Freya nodded at them. "Gavin and Jim," she said. "Thusly named to keep them grounded. It's not working."

Wren laughed, and together they headed into the house.

* * *

Tilladrum had been home to the Struthers clan forever, and before even stepping over the threshold Wren knew what to expect.

The three As.

Antlers.

Ancestors.

Antiques.

Yup.

To which she could add another, she realised, following Wren down a long stone-floored passageway. *Armour.*

Wren also saw several fireplaces that were big enough to stand up in, some tantalising glimpses of ancient tartan carpet, lots of faded old tapestries, and acres of wood panelling.

"In here," Freya said after a while, motioning Wren to follow.

It was the library. Floor-to-ceiling bookshelves going all the way around the room, each shelf crammed with gilt-edged leather volumes, and a large table in the centre laden with piles of books and various ink and watercolour spreads showing early blueprints, sketches and planting schemes for the walled garden.

"Wow…" said Wren. "May I?"

Freya spread her hands. "Please. All yours. Jasper dug all these out. He's got that whole bookish, curatorial – I mean, what I'm saying is – *nerd* thing going on. He'll take you through it all. He should be here in a few minutes."

"Great," said Wren. "There's so much here."

"Yes," said Freya. "I think it was my great-great-great-grandmother who commissioned all these. And she made sketches and watercolours of her own, too, see?"

Freya passed Wren some beautiful old watercolour renderings of the walled garden soon after it was constructed. "Aren't they lovely? And she was a great plantswoman, apparently."

"They are. They're amazing. Thanks, Freya. They're exactly what I need."

"Great. Well, the library and everything in it is at your disposal, Wren. Come and go as suits, okay?"

"Thanks, Freya. All this is just great. It's going to help me so much."

Freya smiled widely. "Brilliant. Have you met Seamus yet, by the way?"

The question took Wren by surprise, and she could only hope her *open book of a face*, as her dad called it, hadn't given too much away.

She tugged her ear.

"Seamus? We, um, yesterday we, um. Yeah. Yes, I mean, we met yesterday."

Never mind her face. Her words weren't exactly coming together in any useful or meaningful capacity, either.

Both of which Freya seemed to pick up on.

"He…" Freya smiled. She seemed to be searching for the right phrasing herself. "He can be a little bit…"

"Rude?" Wren offered.

Freya looked past Wren and into the middle distance, again seemingly searching for the right words.

"Well," she began, "yes, a little... *spiky*," she said. "A little *abrasive*. At first."

"Yes," said Wren. "I get the sense he prefers his own company."

"That's true," she said. "Yes, that's Seamus. At least for now, anyway. Silence and solitude over conversation and company."

Another smile.

"Like I say. Spiky. A bit of a wounded bear."

Wren nodded.

"I got that vibe."

And then some, she added silently.

"He lost his wife, you see. And he... it's taking time..."

"Oh," said Wren, "in that case, yes, I see. Of course..."

Freya smiled. "Wounded bear or not, however," she said, "I'm afraid he's going to have to come out of his cave for a bit because I'm hoping you two might be able to put your heads together on something for me."

Put their heads together? *Her and Seamus?*

Wren's insides caved a little.

"Oh?" said Wren.

"Yes," said Freya. "Rather a nice little project, too. A little mini overhaul of the glasshouse in the walled garden in time for a wedding magazine shoot I've lined up. It could result in a much-needed boost to our bookings for next year."

"Right," said Wren. "Sounds interesting." She faltered a polite smile, even though her mind was already busy replaying Seamus's *back-off-and-keep-out-of-my-way-Wendy* monologue.

"Sounds really, really... interesting..."

Chapter Eight

A long day. A back-breaking day. A day of hacking and clearing and wheelbarrowing and also plucking interesting finds out of the soil.

But with luck, the hot bath Wren had taken, and the good night's sleep she planned on having, would see off the worst of the aches in her arms, back and shoulders.

She yawned and snuggled deeper into her covers to start composing a message to her dad. She'd barely checked in with him since she arrived.

She glanced at Herbert bear, bandaged now, and seated on a chair in the corner of her bedroom.

Yes. A missive from Herbert would do the trick.

She began typing.

> Officer Herbert bear reporting for duty, sir.
>
> I trust you are well?
>
> I myself am a little shaken, sir, having endured a rather perilous encounter with a crow, you see.
>
> The blighter lifted me clean into the air and made off with me. I do believe the reprobate had its eye on my stuffing for a nest.

Fortunately, our mutual friend was able to trace my whereabouts to a copse of woodland nearby and effect a rescue.

Much to my relief, I might add.

And speaking of our mutual friend, sir, she is quite well. Quite well. Her accommodation is most agreeable, and she is most excited to progress her work in the garden.

One potential spanner in the works, however, sir, is the presence of a rather gruff chap who looks after the woodland on the estate. Our mutual friend and he appear not to have quite hit it off, I am afraid.

Perhaps in time, the situation will improve, sir, and the gruff chap may concede one or two words of conversation here and there. I do hope so, sir. However, I must speak plainly: our mutual friend is feeling rather peeved with the fellow.

For my part, sir, I wish to reserve judgement. You see, sir, I believe he may have had a hand in my rescue. I cannot be exactly sure. I am afraid I was only semi-conscious at the time. However, it is my hunch that he may have helped to safeguard me at a crucial moment in the proceedings. For which, naturally, I am most grateful.

Our mutual friend is, as I write, very nearly asleep, sir. Therefore I, too, shall turn in.

A very good night to you, sir. And again, please be assured that all is quite well here at Tilladrum.

Your faithful servant,

Herbert bear

Wren attached a photo to the message – of Herbert bear sporting a thick bandage around his middle – and hit *send*.

She stared into the middle distance for a long moment.

Maybe she'd judged Seamus a little too hastily.

She didn't mind *gruff* too much – if the person underneath the gruffness was... *decent*.

But how do you find out if someone is decent – if they won't talk to you?

"Riddle me *that*, Seamus," she mumbled, turning off her phone.

There was something else. A minor niggle bedding in at the back of Wren's mind.

If Seamus wouldn't talk to her... and if he refused to *work* with her, which was a distinct possibility... If she really *was* largely left to her own devices – was she going to go quietly mad here at Tilladrum?

She glanced across the room again at Herbert bear, bandaged up to the nines for the purposes of her daft communiqués to her dad.

"Madness. Yes. Also a distinct possibility," Wren murmured, sleepily aware of her eyelids fluttering shut, and the soft, soft pillows under her head. "Going quietly mad at Tilladrum," she murmured sleepily, "is definitely a *distinct* possibility..."

Chapter Nine

The calendar.

Seamus was staring at it – as he did every morning.

It was pinned to the wall beside the window in his kitchen, and every morning while he drank his bitter black coffee, his eyes dragged themselves to a new square.

A *different date.*

It was an exercise in registering the inevitable churn of the days.

One after the other after the other.

A meditation on life's brutal forward momentum.

A meditation on how every single day carried him further and further from... *that* day... while at the same time bringing him all the way back to it again.

Just one whole year later.

One year.

Two years.

Three.

And – as of today – *four.*

The twenty-seventh day of March four years ago.

The day Jane left him.

The day Jane died.

He bowed his head and closed his eyes.

Braced his hands against the kitchen table for a long moment.

And when he opened his eyes again, he saw the light had gone out of the sky and been replaced with pewter-black clouds, heavy with the promise of rain.

Good, Seamus thought, gathering his things.

Good.

Chapter Ten

Wren and Seamus were standing side by side outside the glasshouse in the walled garden.

"What do you think?" Freya was saying, her eyes going a little anxiously from Wren to Seamus and Seamus to Wren.

"You'd be helping me out *so* much if you could put your heads together and spruce it up and, you know, work some kind of garden-y woodland-y collaborative magic on it."

"We've got..." Freya pulled out her phone and tapped at it for a few seconds, "...three weeks. Is that enough?"

Wren darted a look at Seamus.

Stony.

Unreadable.

Rude.

"I mean, it just needs to work photographically, you know?" Freya continued. "I realise you can't overhaul it significantly. And in any case, it doesn't want to be too restored. Too perfect. You know?"

Seamus slid a sideways look at Wren.

Impressive, Wren thought, to be able to pack so much hostility into a mere glance. It wouldn't have surprised her if he'd followed up the look with a growl.

Freya gave them both one of her wide, lovely smiles. "I think it could work. Do you?" she said hopefully.

Wren's heart sank.

"The thing is, Freya," Wren began, swallowing, and returning Seamus's dark look with a look of her own. She was aiming for flinty. She couldn't be sure that she'd nailed it though.

"...the thing is, I just wonder if it might not be the *best*–"

"We'd be very happy to help out, Freya," Seamus cut in, verbally trampling over Wren's tentative effort to extricate both of them from anything that could be deemed *collaboration*.

"It won't be any problem at all," Seamus said, turning to Wren.

"Will it Wren?"

Wren opened her mouth. Then closed it again.

"I... No." She forced a smile. "No. Yes. I mean, no problem. It won't. At all."

"Awesome!" Freya said, clapping her hands together. "And apologies, but I'm already late for another meeting."

Wren watched Freya go, then turned back to Seamus to get this whole thing nailed down.

Only thing was, Seamus was already halfway up the hill to the woods.

* * *

It was a bit sneaky of her, but Freya couldn't resist ducking behind an outbuilding and peering back to see if Wren and Seamus were duking it out or forming an alliance.

Oh. *Ah*. Neither of the above, she noted, seeing Wren alone in front of the glasshouse, distractedly checking the opening and closing mechanism of one of the shutters – and Seamus striding powerfully back up the hill.

Hmmm. "No love lost between *these* two," she mumbled to herself, but followed it up with a smile.

"*Yet*."

She resumed a brisk walk back to the house. She just... she had a *feeling* about the two of them, and she couldn't shake it.

But, she did this. Not unlike the island's senior matchmaker, Elspeth McGillicuddy, Freya occasionally became slightly obsessive about getting people together. But hey. She *was* in the wedding business. She believed in love.

Do you though? queried a voice in her head.

Do you? When it comes to yourself?

Freya marched on ahead, ignoring it.

Pfft. Maybe. *Once.* Okay? she fired back, albeit again, in her head.

She *had* believed in true love once. Had believed in *The One...* Once.

But, like all the other once-upon-a-times she'd grown up with, *that* concept – the big idea about The One – had for her, at least, long ago been permanently filed under *Fairytales.*

That's where it belonged. And that's where it would stay.

True love was for *others.* True love was for the ones she made *The Big Day* special for. She cared about that, and she was good at it. And, thankfully, it helped her pay the bills every month.

She, however, was just meant to be on her own, and she'd made her peace with that.

If it left her with a small ache in her chest from time to time, so be it.

She could live with a small ache.

Not a problem.

Chapter Eleven

Pounding.

Pounding. On her front door.

Wren quickly dried her hands and rushed to the front hall to open it.

Seamus.

What was he doing here?

He looked at her with a deadpan expression, then handed her a woven trug overflowing with green leaves.

"Wild garlic," he said. "Sauté it in a bit of butter," he shrugged. "Wilt it down like spinach. That sort of thing."

Wren's mouth had fallen open a bit.

He looked over her shoulder then and frowned.

"I'm sorry," he said, bringing his eyes back to hers. "For the other day."

It started to rain.

"I was rude to you. And I'm sorry."

He stood there, apparently not even noticing the rain.

Wren looked down at the trug, and the heaped greens spilling over its sides.

"D'you want to come in for a minute?" she said, "wait for the rain to stop?"

To Wren's surprise, he shrugged and said. "Yeah, okay."

* * *

To Wren's further surprise, that minute turned into a couple of hours.

Wren put some pieces of chicken to roast in the oven, and Seamus took care of sautéing the wild garlic – which was delicious, actually – and soon enough, the two of them were chatting quite companionably about getting started on the glasshouse together the following day.

"Turns out you're not a bad cook," he said with a mischievous grin as he was heading off.

Wren laughed.

"Turns out you're... not as offensive as I first thought," Wren fired back.

"Touché," said Seamus, still with that grin.

Wren felt herself swoon a tiny bit. He had the warmest, most handsome smile she'd seen in a very long time.

She walked him to the door.

"Still raining."

"Yeah. To be honest, I don't mind the rain."

"I know," she said. "I've noticed."

"Have you now?"

That smile of his again – giving way to a slightly more serious expression.

"So here's the deal. I'm going to try not to be such an idiot, going forward. And also," he added, walking to the gate, calling over his shoulder, "it's good to have you around. Wendy."

She shook her head at him but she was smiling.

"Thanks," she laughed. "I'll see you tomorrow."

He was still smiling too.

"Yeah," he said. "See you tomorrow."

* * *

Instead of heading straight to bed after her bath, Wren returned to the kitchen table.

Her mind was too busy to fall asleep easily, even if her arms ached from the day's work.

She brought out her tray of finds from the garden – lots of little bits of glass. Lots of little pieces of broken crockery – and she sat for a long while just sifting and sorting through them until her mind quietened and her eyelids grew heavy.

Eventually, she stood and stretched and blew out her candles.

And out of the window, up the hill, from somewhere deep in the woods, she made out a curl of woodsmoke rising from Seamus's cottage.

Chapter Twelve

They were a pretty good team, as it turned out.

In the space of two weeks, Wren and Seamus took the Victorian glasshouse from semi-derelict to, well, quite spruce.

Seamus made repairs to the window frames and got the wooden shutters working again. Wren cleaned up the original tiles and cast iron floor grilles and tamed the trailing ivy to the point of pretty, as opposed to rampant.

And by the time Freya popped in to see what they'd done, the place was looking lovely.

"I can't believe it," she said. "I *cannot* believe that you've got it looking so good. Thank you. Thank you both so much."

Seamus smiled as he watched her go. "I think she's happy."

Wren smiled too. "I think she is," she said. "They've got a lot on their hands, with this place, haven't they?"

Seamus gave a long, low whistle. "You can say that again."

Wren angled her head. "How long have you been at Tilladrum, Seamus?"

Although the couple of weeks they'd spent working together hadn't yielded a *lot* of conversation, Wren was by now at least a little more comfortable with asking Seamus the occasional question.

"About a year," he said. "It was just one of those random things. A chance conversation. Friend of a friend of a friend sort of thing. Someone I know knows someone who knows Freya. And you know what Freya's like. She is to the battered souls among us as the flame is to the moth."

Wren laughed. "Yes. That chimes. In my case, my dad – and you know, I don't even know how or where now that I come to think of it – but my dad got hold of a flyer advertising for an enthusiastic volunteer, basically, to come and live in Gardener's Cottage and kick things off in the walled garden."

"And you'd no qualms?" Seamus said, "You just fancied upping sticks and coming out here?"

Wren shook her head. "I couldn't get here fast enough, once it occurred to me I had no reason not to come."

Seamus was looking at her in a way that suggested he was too polite, or reserved, to probe her further.

She smiled at him. A sad rather than a glad smile.

Well. May as well tell him.

"I was jilted, Seamus. Left standing at the altar," she said. "My husband-to-be left me on our wedding day."

Seamus stopped what he was doing.

"You're joking."

Wren laughed. And then nearly cried. And then laughed again.

"I'm not. I am *that* woman."

Seamus wheeled away and wheeled back again and swore under his breath for a few long moments.

And that made Wren feel inexplicably and massively *better* about things.

"What an absolute a–" he paused, corrected himself, "*idiot*," he said, shaking his head again, and swearing again under his breath.

"Yeah. Not... stand-up guy behaviour, really, is it..."

"No. No, it's not." Seamus was still shaking his head, and looking at her like he was seeing her differently. "Not by a long shot."

Wren found herself becoming a little – *what*? – embarrassed? *Shy?* She wasn't really sure – under Seamus's intense gaze.

"Hey. It's fine. It's four – actually, nearly five months ago now. You'd be surprised how quickly you can fall out of love with someone when you realise they're actually quite a callous, unfeeling, a–"

"Idiot," Seamus supplied, with a smile and a raised brow.

Wren returned his smile. "Yeah. *Idiot*."

She shook her head a little. "It's... I don't know. I feel like I'm experiencing some sort of emotional whiplash. I go round in circles with it. I thought he was *The One*."

Seamus was listening. Quietly and intently. Just listening. And Wren suddenly realised how much talking about it all felt... good.

"I mean," she continued, "now I very definitely know that he *wasn't*. But... it's unsettling. It makes you realise... or makes you wonder... can you ever really be sure...?"

She was again struck by the fact that Seamus was a good listener.

"Wren. You were left standing at the altar. He left you on your wedding day. It doesn't surprise me at all that you were left wondering... who is this guy?"

"Well, yeah..." Wren agreed. "Anyway..."

She turned away from Seamus at that moment and walked to one of the tall and, presently, open windows.

"Oh. Hello," she said, to a robin that had stationed himself on the sill outside.

Seamus wandered over to join her.

"Morning, little man," he said.

The robin cocked its head and hopped a bit closer to him.

Wren turned to Seamus, a quizzical look on her face. "Wait. You speak robin?"

Seamus raised his eyebrows and gave her one of his looks. "Course I do. What sort of woodsman would I be if I didn't speak robin?"

"Why?" he said, eyeing her sideways. "Do you?"

"Of course I do. I mean I speak *bear*. What sort of bear-whisperer doesn't also speak robin?"

Seamus grinned at her, then chuckled, then nodded.

"Fair play. Fair play. Well, that's something we have in common, then," he smiled. "We both speak robin."

Wren smiled back, and once again registered his tousled dark hair, and his kind, handsome face.

She felt a little flare of something. A little spark. Because something had passed between them just now. Something that had her looking at him in a slightly different light. And, she sensed, had him looking at *her* in some kind of different light, too.

She watched, smiling on in amusement, while he conducted a lengthy and elaborate robin-speak conversation with their feathered visitor. And she did what she could to resist the appeal of his wide, mischievous smile. But it wasn't easy. Because Seamus and his wide, mischievous smiles were increasingly sending little flutters through her. *Flutters. Butterflies*, for goodness' sake.

What was she? Fourteen?

She tried to ignore them. Tried to focus on the robin. But it was no use. The robin wasn't cutting it. The robin wasn't distracting her from revisiting the thought that she was seeing something new in Seamus. And this, in itself, prompted another thought

What about him? she wondered. Was he seeing her in a different light these days? Or was he still just hugely, if these days more discreetly, annoyed by her presence?

By *her*?

Who knew? Warm, handsome smiles aside, Seamus was a closed book.

Wren could only hope that if he *was* feeling something else, something *different*, that it wasn't pity.

She just really, really hoped it wasn't pity.

Chapter Thirteen

A good week, sir. A very good week.

Our mutual friend and the woodsman, having got off on rather the wrong foot, now appear to be very much more on the right foot.

Or, feet, if you prefer, sir? Foot, feet, regardless – they are no longer squabbling, and indeed they have these past two weeks collaborated on a most successful stretch of days in the Orangery at Tilladrum. I gather the lady of the house is most pleased with the results, and plans to offer the use of space to her wedding clients and whatnot.

But if I may return to the subject of our mutual friend and this woodsman, sir. Between you, me and the gatepost, well, I daresay that if things were not as they are, one could quite see the young lady falling for this chap.

However, our mutual friend has been wrangling with this matter for some days now, sir, and has just this morning made it very plain to me that since things are what they are, there shall be no falling.

No, sir. I am reliably informed that there shall be
no falling of any kind, whatsoever.

Our mutual friend is most insistent that civility
and professionalism are the order of the day
when it comes to The Woodsman.

Nothing more. Nothing less.

Wren sighed and put her phone down. She was finding it too difficult to channel Herbert right now. Or just too difficult to put into words whatever it was she was trying to say.

And *that*, she concluded, was probably heavily tied up in the fact that her feelings were in a horrible tangle and she was having trouble unravelling them.

She looked out of the window for a long time instead.

In a series of recent talks with herself, she had tried to press home the need to park the crush she'd been forming on Seamus.

She couldn't be getting crushes on people. On widowers for goodness' sake!

She was only four months on from the abrupt rug-pull of the relationship she'd thought was the defining relationship of her life.

Why was she falling in l–

She shut *that* question down.

Why was she developing *crushes* on people?

She needed to batten down her emotional hatches.

She needed space.

She needed, clearly, to be alone, and to steer clear of the guy up the hill.

Chapter Fourteen

~~~~

"That's right, yeah..."

Seamus. Seamus's lovely Irish brogue carrying through the trees.

"...the green wood's much easier to work with the hand tools. I think you'll be surprised to see what you can get done in just a few days."

Wren clenched her teeth in a *yikes* and about-turned.

She'd forgotten about the workshops.

Working with green wood. Whittling. That sort of thing. Seamus and Jasper had come up with them as a way to generate some additional income for the estate. Three-and-four-day workshops to fill the gaps in the calendar between wedding bookings.

It was okay, she thought. *No one had seen her.* She'd just scoot back down the hill and hang out at home.

Watching the waves crashing on the west beach would have to wait for another day. As would Herbert's hilltop photoshoot.

"Wren."

She froze.

Seamus.

Calling her name.

What was wrong with her? Why was she behaving like this?

Because she—

Because—

Because being near him was making her feel...

Yes. Bingo. *That*. Just *that* Being near him was making her *feel*. And she hadn't come to Tilladrum to *feel*. She'd come to Tilladrum to retreat and repair and rebuild.

She didn't want feelings. Not unless they were about plants.

All the other feelings could do one. She didn't want them. She didn't want *any* of them.

"Wren..."

Seamus again. She turned on her heel and began walking briskly back the way she'd come.

No. No, no, no...

Footfall. His. Behind her.

"Hey..."

His voice was low. Gentle.

Wren stopped. She closed her eyes for a second. And then she turned around.

"Oh, hi!" Her voice sounded false. Too bright. "Sorry," she went on. "I didn't mean to interrupt. I forgot you were running a workshop and when I stumbled across you all there, I thought I'd better just... you know... slip away unnoticed."

Seamus was watching her. Studying her quite intently.

"You're good," he said. "You're not interrupting."

Wren smiled awkwardly. And was then dismayed to find she was following up the awkward smile with an even more awkward silence.

Seamus waited for her to say something. When she didn't, he spoke instead.

"Haven't seen you for a while."

He was studying her very intently, in a way that made her tummy flip.

"You been okay?"

She swallowed.

And Seamus continued to study her.

"Me?" There it was again. The overly-bright voice. "Oh, yeah. You know. Just... Busy..."

Seamus nodded slowly, searching her face for the meaning underneath the too-bright-sounding small talk.

"Right. Cause... I wanted to thank you."

Wren must have looked a little confused.

"For the thing," he smiled. "The thing you left on the gatepost last week." He smiled again, a little apologetically. "I mean, what would you call it?"

Wren returned his smile. Ah. *Yes.* It occurred to her now that an explanatory note to go with the *thing* would have been a good idea.

"It's a light catcher," she said quietly, aware that she was searching his face, now. Aware too, she realised, with a small sharp pang, that she'd missed his face. That she'd missed *him*.

"I make them," she went on. "You just... hang it in your window..." she laughed a little bit, "so that, you know, it catches the light."

Seamus gave her another one of his smiles. "A light catcher," he said. "That's... Thanks. Thank you."

Wren nodded.

She'd made one for her kitchen window out of the bits of glass she'd pulled from the earth in the walled garden. And on a whim, she'd made one for Seamus, too.

"That's okay," she said. "In return for the wild garlic."

Their eyes locked and, not for the first time, something wordless passed, *sparked*, between them.

And it was too much.

And it was not okay.

Because Wren knew she was likely rebounding horribly right now. How could she not be?

And he – the poor guy – was mourning his wife and–

Just... None of this was okay. None of this... *worked*.

"Anyway," she said, turning to leave, "I should go..."

"Don't," he said. "Don't go."

His face was all kindness and sincerity and her insides just caved.

"Stay for a bit. Come on."

He stretched out his hand, his eyes all smiling and kind. "You're kind of obliged to," he said. "Cause I've told this lot all about you."

Wren looked over his shoulder to where a handful of men and women were milling about under the tarpaulin Seamus had rigged up.

Against her better judgement, she relented. She took his hand. And did what she could to ignore the butterflies taking flight in her belly.

"Marga and Jill? Carlo and Rafe?" Seamus called, "This is my friend, Wren. The girl I was telling you about."

"The one that speaks bear?" one of the group called over.

"That's the one," Seamus grinned, darting her a mischievous look. "That's the one."

Wren blushed a bit and laughed. Then she followed Seamus back up to the clearing.

It didn't escape her notice that he kept hold of her hand for a fraction longer than he needed to.

Chapter Fifteen

By the time the sun was setting behind the woods and Seamus's students had one-by-one said their goodbyes and drifted off towards Tilladrum to sample Jasper's cooking, Wren and Seamus found themselves side by side in the clearing.

The birds were quieting. All that could be heard was the stirring of the leaves in the trees and the distant, rhythmic crash of waves in the bay far below.

Wren felt Seamus's eyes settle on her.

"Do you think," she said, holding a small object in front of her face, the better to inspect it, "I have potential as a carpenter? Or, let's say, a whittler?"

Seamus came closer and gently took the object she'd been carving all afternoon from her hands.

She tried to ignore the fact that the brush of his fingers against hers stirred those butterflies again.

"I think," he began, "I *think* you'd bring a very avant-garde if not plain *wonky* sensibility to the craft," he said, holding up the misshapen piece of wood and turning it around for a full inspection. "Don't you?"

They both laughed.

"I think you might be right."

They locked eyes for a moment, both of them still smiling.

"Hey," Seamus said, "I've a stew that needs eating. And I've several *classic* board games that need playing. And, look, though I wouldn't *dream* of trying to sway you in any way, my collection includes the much-underrated and generally vastly overlooked *Guess Who?*"

Wren had to laugh. "You're kidding me," she said. "I absolutely love that game! I used to play it with my dad all the time."

Seamus smiled broadly.

"Okay then," he said. "I think that seals the deal. That, plus the fact that I'm both a witty and charming host, no doubt."

Wren raised an eyebrow at him and he laughed.

"You're right. I'm just plain bad at conversation. In fact, I'm just plain bad at social interaction in general. As I believe you are aware. But..." he smiled at her, and added quietly, "I'm trying."

Wren fought off a sudden urge to hug him and tell him how sorry she was for all that he'd lost, and the grief he'd been plunged into, and the unfairness of it all.

She couldn't imagine what he'd been through. *What he was still going through.*

But she also had to think about her own bruised heart. And the whole point of her coming to Tilladrum. Which had been to retreat. To heal. To recover. Not to... not to fall–

She cut that *thought off at the pass.*

Yeah. You should say no, she told herself. *You should politely decline.* You should say *no,* and you should keep things uncomplicated.

She opened her mouth to speak.

"That sounds good," she said.

Gah. Wren. No, chided the self-protective voice in her head. *This is not wise. This is not wise at all.*

"That sounds really, really good."

* * *

Seamus stole a glance or two at Wren as they walked down the hill in a half-companionable, half-slightly-awkward silence, a single thought playing over and over in his mind.

She'd been avoiding him.

He got that now.
He also got *why*.
At least, he was pretty sure he did.
She was scared. She was as scared as he was.

Chapter Sixteen

It had been a good evening, Seamus reflected. A really good evening.

The food had been pretty good, even if he said so himself. And the company had been good, too – that being down to Wren.

Seamus got back to his cottage a little after midnight, having walked Wren down the hill to hers.

"You don't need to walk me home, Seamus," she'd said. "I think I'm pretty safe here..."

And he'd frowned and shaken his head and said, "You've not heard about the big black cat that haunts the Highlands then? The quiet places, in particular?"

"Wh– no?"

"Yep," he'd said. "Big black ghost cat of a thing." And he'd leaned closer at that, adding in a whisper, "Haunts the quiet places. At night."

And Wren had given him one of her cute, kind of quizzical sideways looks, saying, "No. Really? Come on!"

And he'd just smiled all enigmatically, like, and given a little shrug.

And maybe... *maybe*... he realised, on reflection, she'd started walking a tiny bit closer to him.

And maybe... *maybe*, he realised, also on reflection, he'd kind of liked that.

Back in his cottage, he hooked his coat onto a peg inside the front door and wandered back into his kitchen.

The room still held a faint trace of Wren's perfume.

Guess Who was still set up on the table.

How many games had they played? Starting off sensibly enough – Does yours have brown eyes? Is yours wearing a hat? – but the whole thing soon degenerating into a mutual ribbing.

Does yours look like someone with problematic interpersonal skills?

Does yours look like someone who falsifies messages to her father from her childhood teddy bear?

Seamus smiled. Yeah. It had been a good evening. They'd laughed a lot. And it had been a long time since he'd laughed.

He moved to the window. Slowly. Deliberately.

Not to look at the calendar beside it.

Not to reflect on the brutal progress of the days.

No. He'd gone to the window to look again at the light catcher Wren had made for him. He'd hung it there once he'd learned what it was. And sure enough... All its little pieces of jewel-coloured glass were indeed glinting, glowing, reflecting and catching the light.

"Light catcher..." he murmured, feeling a small tug of something in his chest. "I'd say so. I'd definitely say so."

Chapter Seventeen

~~~

Wren sat up in bed, hugging her knees and wiping away fresh tears with the sleeve of her pyjamas.

It had been the best evening. The *most* fun, the *most* laughter, the *best* company she'd had in a very long time.

So why was she crying?

Because she... it sounded so ridiculous. And yet it was what it was. *Because she was falling in love with him.*

Seamus. She was falling *in love* with him.

And what was the point in *that*?

He would never, *could* never, reciprocate that love.

Seamus. Poor, bereaved Seamus. He was still married, *really*.

He was still *in love* with his wife.

Yes, she'd been gone from him for four years. But he still *loved her*.

Of course he did.

He hadn't wanted to leave her. And she, his wife, *Jane*, hadn't wanted to leave *him*.

But she hadn't had any choice in the matter. And nor had Seamus.

And that's what made it so achingly, horribly, heartbreakingly sad.

Seamus's wife had left him. Completely and utterly unwillingly.

And Seamus had never stopped loving her.

And Wren could quite see, could *absolutely* see, why he never would.

And that was love.

That was just... *love*.

And that was why she was crying.

She was falling in love – *had* fallen in love – with someone who couldn't love her back.

Chapter Eighteen

"Sorry, I'm not sure I want to–"

Strange.

Was that her voice? It sounded... far away. And it sounded... yes, *strange*.

Strange was also what she was feeling.

Strange. And *sick*.

It had all happened so fast.

She and Seamus had been helping the photo shoot people from the wedding magazine set up in the glasshouse, bundling in and out with armfuls of wedding dresses, make-up, lights, cameras, tripods, reflector panels, diffuser panels...

And then the phone calls and increasingly agitated voice messages had started, until it emerged that their model had missed her connecting flight.

Urgent back-and-forths had ensued. Seamus had been sent off to the big house on some errand, and Wren had been pulled away from her efforts at re-routing the ivy away from the lighting.

But because she'd been up a ladder and busy with her ivy wrangling, Wren had not been paying a whole lot of attention to the increasingly stressed whispering going on between Alex and Sophie, two of the stylists.

Until she heard her name.

"Wren? *Wren*, is it?" Alex called across the room to her. "Yeah. Wren darlin', could you do us a *massive* favour?"

It was explained to Wren that the model wasn't coming and they were now very, very stuck.

"You're about the right size, love," Sophie said. "Yeah. Other than the height," said Alex. "But that's not a dealbreaker... You'll absolutely do. We'll just use you as a placeholder, yeah? And the designers'll photoshop you out when we're back in London."

"Well, I mean, I..."

Well, I mean, I... The extent, apparently, of Wren's ability to articulate that, no. No, thank you. She wouldn't actually like to be put in a wedding dress. Wouldn't actually like to have to pretend to be a bride. Wouldn't actually like any of that *at all.*

But before Wren could try to formulate a more empowered come-back than *Well, I mean, I...* the two stylists had bundled her down the ladder and started unbuttoning her overalls.

"You're such a star!" Sophie said, dropping a beautiful ivory gown over Wren's head.

"Yeah. Legend," said Alex, tugging it down over her body. "Total lifesaver."

And, life-long people-pleaser that she was, Wren inevitably rolled out the people-pleaser playbook.

"Um, well, okay," she was saying, and "No, I don't mind," and, "It's fine, it's okay, it's no problem..."

Only, the thing was, it really *wasn't* okay. And suddenly, she really *did* mind. And what was more, it really, really *was* a problem.

It was a problem to have been shoved into a wedding dress. It was a *problem* to be plunged without warning into a sickening flashback of *that* day, and *that* moment.

She squeezed her eyes tightly shut, as if that might help.

But no. Whether she wanted to be or not, whether it was *okay* with her or not – she was back there.

Back at St Ninian's. Back at the altar. Never in her life so alone. Never in her life so exposed. And never in her life so humiliated. Or rejected.

She had pushed the memory of that day under the surface again and again and again. Had denied it, ignored it, and even done a passable job of convincing herself it had never happened.

But *what do you know?* Wren thought bitterly. Plonking on a wedding dress and standing all alone inside a beautiful Victorian glasshouse while strangers looked on assessingly and took photographs of her... *That'd do it. That'd do just fine* as a suitable trigger for bringing back the whole sickening day.

For forcing her to face what she had lost.

She felt herself turn very cold. Numb. Like she was seizing up with grief.

Do you see? said a small voice in her head. *Do you see what you lost that day? Are you beginning to grasp that?*

Yes. Cold, numb and stunned, Wren *did* see. She saw her life stretching out ahead of her. And she saw that it was... empty.

She started to shake. The lace collar on the wedding dress was tightening around her neck. She pulled at it. Clawed at it.

She couldn't breathe.

She couldn't remember how.

Small, uneven gulps of air. Was that it? Was that right?

No.

She gulped again.

And again.

It wasn't working.

It didn't feel right.

She didn't feel right.

She tugged again at the lace collar.

Too tight. Still too tight.

She tried to speak to the stylists. To get their attention. But they were looking at their moodboard, and thrashing out the next batch of shots.

"Please..." Wren spluttered. "I can't... I can't seem to breathe..."

Alex and Sophie weren't listening.

No one was listening.

"Please," she said again. "I'm not... I can't–"

But it was no use. Talking was impossible. The glasshouse began to dip and sway and spin – and Wren found that... she found that... she found...

Seamus.

Seamus's eyes. Locked on hers. Wide and dark and full of concern.

And so she let go. She just let go. And the last thing she saw as the world tilted and turned dark at the edges and fell away from under her was *him*, Seamus, moving powerfully across the room towards her, his dark eyes locked firmly on hers.

Chapter Nineteen

In the early afternoon following Wren's morning fainting episode, one of the soon-departing stylists, Alex, called in at her cottage with a handful of insta-printed polaroid-type photographs of Seamus carrying Wren out of the glasshouse.

Wren blinked, then stared at them.

"Très romantique, innit?" the stylist quipped. "The handsome prince carrying sleeping beauty off to a happy-ever-after?"

Wren looked up at her and fought the urge to cry. "You couldn't be more wrong, Alex," she said weakly, handing back the stack of photos.

You couldn't be more catastrophically wrong.

When Alex left, Wren had snuggled down on her sofa under one of Freya's soft tartan blankets and closed her eyes.

When she opened them again, the light was going out of the sky.

She heard a soft knock on her living room door.

"Come in..." she said, sitting up a bit and rubbing her eyes.

It was Seamus. Smiling at her.

"Hi," he said, stepping a little way into the room. "How's the patient?"

Oh, you know, dying. Of embarrassment.

"Hi," she said. "Come in. I'm fine. I'm absolutely fine. And thank you. For today, I mean. I don't remember much–"

She did. She remembered the solid safety of his arms, gathering her up and holding her. She remembered that. She would always remember that.

"–but the stylists told me it's thanks to you I didn't split my head open." He frowned.

"I'm sorry the whole thing happened, Wren. They shouldn't have done that. They shouldn't have put you in that dress, and made you–"

"They weren't to know. I should have just said no. But anyway. It's all fine. No harm done. Thanks to you, mainly – and your well-timed catch."

She smiled at him then, and his smile returned too. She thought he might be about to say something. But the moment passed.

"Okay then," he said instead. "I'll leave you to it."

Wren nodded, folding back the blanket so she could get up and walk him to the door.

"No you don't," he started to say. But she batted it away. "I'm fine," she said, laughing. "I'm fine."

Seamus opened the front door, and the two of them stood there at the threshold for a moment watching the rain patter down.

Seamus hesitated, a muscle working briefly along his jaw. And then he said, "Wren, I wanted to say," his eyes gently settled on hers, "I wanted to say that... I'm here. If you need a friend, like. I'm here. Okay?"

Wren felt tears pricking her eyes, and whether Seamus noticed or not, whether it made a difference or not, he very gently put his arms around her.

She reached around him, too, holding him close, breathing him in.

Woodsmoke. Heather. Soap.

"Okay," she said, before dipping her head and gently extricating herself from his arms.

"Thank you."

Seamus nodded.

"G'night then," he said.

"Good night, Seamus."

She watched him go and saw that at the gate, for the briefest moment, he seemed to hesitate. But then he went on his way towards the hill that would take him up to the woods.

Wren stayed on alone under the shelter of the porch for a time, watching the rain patter down.

When she went back inside to the warmth of her kitchen, she saw a tiny, whittled bird on her table.

Seamus. He must have left it there.

She picked it up and turned it over carefully in her hands.

It was a tiny, whittled wren.

Chapter Twenty

Elspeth McGillicuddy, proprietress of The Gannet's Beak down at Gannet Bay, was killing two birds with one stone in the form of rolling out her new menu and raising funds for one of her charitable causes.

And, Wren had been reliably informed, tonight it was the turn of Tilladrum Estate and all those involved with it to turn up and splash the cash a bit.

"Is attendance, you know, mandatory?" Wren asked Freya.

Freya raised her eyebrows and made a sort of 'o' shape with her mouth.

"Is it mandatory," she repeated, looking into the middle distance and furrowing her brow. "Um, I mean... no? But also, I think, really, yes? If that helps?"

It didn't.

Wren nodded. "Okay. I think I understand."

She'd have to go. And maybe that was a good thing. She'd been avoiding everyone for a few weeks, avoiding Seamus, particularly. Perhaps this would be an easy way to just... clear the air, or move things on, or just... reboot a little bit.

She'd just needed some time by herself. And as Herbert bear had said, via her dad, of course, sometimes a bit of one's own company is just the ticket.

Wren was aware, though, that a person can have too much of a good thing. Certainly, in her case, there was such a thing as *too much of her own company.*

She'd kept busy in the garden, of course. But other than that, she'd also been spending just about every waking moment coming up with all the reasons why letting herself fall for Seamus was a terrible, terrible idea.

The problem was she was just finding it very difficult to deny what she *felt* whenever he looked at her with his dark, intense eyes. And finding it difficult to stop replaying his words – not that there were many, to be honest – over and over again.

His low-timbre voice. His Dublin brogue.

Worst of all, she was finding it difficult, if not impossible, to stop thinking about his smile, and about the exact way his lips curved into that smile whenever she said something that amused him. Or whenever he said something he knew would amuse *her.*

Just... she had to stop. *It* had to stop. Her... *attraction*... to him. She had to put a stop to it all.

Seamus was off-limits.

Seamus was a no-go.

Her phone *pinged.*

Speak of the devil. It was a text. From *him.*

Swing by at 8pm to pick you up for the Gannet's Beak thing...

Oh no. *But of course.* The car she used here was in for its service.

She swallowed. Then typed, *ok.*

Chapter Twenty-One

Something Wren had said. He'd played the words over and over again in his mind.

It'd started as a nothing sort of chat. Your favourite this. Your least favourite that. Until they'd turned to the seasons. *What's your favourite season?* He'd asked her. And she'd said Spring. And he'd said, right, okay. Why?

And she'd said–

Seamus had to take a moment. Whenever he went back to this, he had to take a moment. He braced his hands on the table, and looked up at the little light catcher, moving a bit in the draught. And, of course, catching the light.

He went back to the conversation:

What's your favourite season, Wren? He'd asked her.

And she'd said, *Spring.*

Why? He'd asked her.

And she'd turned to him, her face so open and lovely and... *good*... and she'd said, *Because it reminds me of the beauty of the world. And the resilience of everything.*

Seamus wiped away a tear.

Then he swallowed.

He looked up at the light catcher for a long moment. Then he looked down at his hand.

And finally, knowing it was the right thing, and knowing that Jane would want him to, he took off his wedding ring.

Chapter Twenty-Two

The event at The Gannet's Beak was in full swing by the time they arrived.

There was a big folk jam happening in the back, and over the noise of fiddles and accordions, Wren could make out the sounds of an auction being conducted off to the side of the little bistro.

They were greeted by Mrs McGillicuddy at the door.

Seamus handed her a fifty-pound note. "Not sure how long we'll be staying, Elspeth. So I'm giving you this now..."

"Ahhhhh! How kind you are! Thank you!" Mrs McGillicuddy leaned towards them both conspiratorially. "And if I may say so," she said, "the pair of you make a very handsome couple!"

Wren's cheeks flamed. She didn't know where to look. So she looked at the floor.

Seamus looked at the floor briefly, too.

"We're not–" Wren began.

But Seamus beat her to it, looking up abruptly, and speaking over her. "We're not a couple, Mrs McGillicuddy," he said, his face dark and unreadable.

"What's that dear?" Mrs McGillicuddy shouted, trying to make herself heard over the music.

"I said we're not a couple," Seamus shot back loudly, before stalking off into the crowd.

* * *

Wren was sitting on the cold damp sand hugging her knees and swiping at tears that just wouldn't stop falling.

"Are you okay?" asked a gentle voice, a woman's voice.

Wren looked up, quickly wiping away a fresh spill of tears.

The owner of the voice was a woman in her thirties with a tumble of dark hair all about her shoulders.

Wren nodded. "I'm fine," she said. "Really. I'm just taking five."

The woman studied her for a moment, trying to place her. "Have I seen you up at Tilladrum? Are you the new gardener?"

Wren nodded.

"I thought I recognised you," she said with a smile. "I'm Rose. I help out with the wedding photography from time to time."

"Right..." Wren said, nodding again. "I see."

"You here for the auction?"

"Yes," Wren managed. "I'll probably go back in in a minute. I just need... some air."

The woman smiled. "Okay. Well, come and find me, if you'd like? If you feel like some company? Or... if you want to talk or anything?"

Wren smiled and nodded.

"That's kind of you. Thanks."

Rose smiled. "Take care, okay?"

Again, Wren nodded. "Yeah. Thanks, Rose."

Kind as Rose's offer was, Wren preferred to stay where she was, just listening to the rhythmic hush and swish of the waves.

And anyway... How could she go back in there?

A couple.

A handsome couple.

She closed her eyes. She'd wanted the ground to swallow her. Poor Seamus, having to hear that. *Having to–*

"Wren."

It was him. It was Seamus. Standing behind her.

Wren scrambled to her feet, immediately backing away from him and swiping at her tear-streaked cheeks.

"I'm sorry," he said. "I don't know why Elspeth said that. Why she had us paired off like that. I don't know why she thought that."

Wren stiffened and backed away from him a step further still.

"I know, right?" she said, hating the quiver in her voice, the emotion laying itself bare there, and her dignity... *dying a death there.*

"Who in their right mind would want to be in a couple with *me?*"

She turned. And she ran.

"Wait!" Seamus called. "Wren! Come back! That's not what I said," he yelled. "And it's not what I meant, either!"

Chapter Twenty-Three

Seamus closed the distance between them in a few long sprints.

"Hey," he said quietly when he'd caught up with her. "Wren. Hey…"

He touched her shoulder gently and she whirled around to face him.

"Would you leave me, Seamus!" she said. "Would you please just leave me!"

He looked confused.

"No," he fired back after a beat, his brows all pulled together in a frown. "No, I won't leave you. Not like this."

"I don't want your *pity*," Seamus, she shouted. "Believe me. I've had enough *pity* from enough *people* to last me several lifetimes. I don't need yours as well."

"Who said anything about pity? I'm trying to apologise. For someone else's insensitivity! When Elspeth said that – all I could think was that it would hurt you. Given everything that's happened. Given everything you've been through. And when I saw your face – when I saw how crestfallen and sad and… hurt… you looked, I went inside to find Freya and tell her I was gonna take you home."

"Wh– You did?"

"Yeah. Why – what did you think I was doing?"

"I thought you were angry. Or upset. About the couple thing. Because of your… because of…"

"Because of Jane?"

Wren nodded.

"Oh," he said. "Okay. I see that. I get that."

"Were you?"

"Was I what?"

"Upset."

"Not for myself, no. But yeah. I was pretty upset and, yeah, a bit angry. On your behalf."

He took a step closer to her.

"And then I find you out here," he frowned, "borderline hypothermic..." He pulled his sweater over his head and wrapped it round her shoulders. "...borderline hypothermic and bawling your eyes out which, in fairness, endorses both my upset *and* my anger."

Wren turned away from him and looked out to sea. There was a tiny light, from some distant ship, blinking on the horizon.

She would tell him. Just tell him. And then she would leave.

"I'm going to tell you why I got so upset, Seamus," she said, turning back to face him. "Then I'm going to apologise. And then I'm going to leave."

She closed her eyes and took a breath. "I got upset back there because... for a long time now... for what *feels* like a really long time, I've been... loving you. I've been falling in love with you and missing you and wanting you and–"

She opened her eyes again and saw Seamus looking at her in that intense way of his, his brows all pulled together, his eyes all dark and concerned.

"–and I'm so sorry. That's why I've been avoiding you. And that's why I'm going to tell Freya I'm leav–"

"Wren."

"I know. I'm sorry. And I apologise," she said. "You're grieving, and you're sad, and the *last*, the *last* thing you need is *me*. Behaving like *this*."

"Wren," Seamus said again. "I'd like to say something now."

"No." Wren shook her head. "No. I won't let you. It's not your job right now to smooth this over and make me feel better for being a complete–"

"Wren," Seamus said, more emphatically now. "Be quiet for one minute."

Wren opened her mouth to protest. Then shut it.

"Before Jane died," said Seamus, "she told me things. She *said* things.

Things like, *you'll meet someone. You'll find someone. You'll fall in love again. Don't underestimate the heart's capacity to love..."* Seamus looked down for a moment. And then he brought his eyes back to Wren. "And I didn't believe her. I *refused* to believe her. For a long, long time. I can be stubborn, like that, believe it or not."

Wren smiled, and Seamus continued. "And, oh, was I stubborn. That's why I came here. To Tilladrum. So that I could be alone. So that I could pull away from the world."

He looked briefly out to sea again, and Wren did too. The small distant light was still blinking there.

"Full disclosure," he said, turning to face her again. "I wasn't... I didn't want... I wasn't *looking,* Wren. I was not looking."

He shook his head. But he continued to look at her. "And then you came along, see, and..."

He paused, and scrubbed a hand over his face for a moment, trying to find the words. "You came along and... you made me feel again. You made me *feel* again. And all I've found myself wanting is to be near you. Just be near you. Be in your presence. See you smile. Hear you laugh."

Wren swiped at the tears falling down her cheeks.

"Talk nonsense with you in the garden. Play those stupid board games with you 'til two in the morning. All of it. All of it, Wren. Just to be around you."

He stepped close enough that he was able to thumb away some of her tears.

"And I've wanted to hold you," he said, looking at her like his heart might break. "And..." he swallowed, "and I've wanted to kiss you."

"Seamus," Wren said, quietly, barely audibly, "I didn't know. I didn't know any of this."

Seamus lowered his head again and stepped closer to her still. "There is no way I could *not* have fallen for you, Wren," he said. He brought his eyes to hers again. "And I don't know what else to tell you."

Wren couldn't speak. Or even really breathe. *Was this real?* Had he really just said all those things? A few minutes ago she was picturing herself back in Reading, sobbing into her cereal.

She looked at him. Really looked at him. And he smiled at her. She knew, then. *She felt it.* It was a smile for her. For her, and no one else.

Seamus reached for her hands. Wren looked down at their fingers locking together. And she saw that his ring wasn't there any more.

So she turned her face up to his. And she kissed him. The gentlest, sweetest of kisses. The one she'd waited for. And, she got the sense, the one he'd waited for too.

They walked back along the beach, her head against his shoulder, his arm around her waist, the distant light far out at sea twinkling back at them, and the waves hushing and shushing their ancient story onto the soft sand.

And Seamus pulled her close, and very quietly said, "You're the beauty of the world and the resilience of everything, Wren. You're Spring."

Chapter Twenty-Four

~∞~

Colin Collett topped up his teapot with freshly boiled water, seated himself at his kitchen table, and returned to his task – which was stuffing half a dozen packets of *Percy Pigs* into a large padded envelope.

He sealed it and was just turning it over to address it when he heard a little *ping* from his phone.

He set the envelope and pen to one side and reached into his pocket.

Ping again.

"Ah," he said, smiling. "Good. Field Operative Herbert bear."

He opened the message and began to read.

> Well, sir, Spring is very much in the air here at Tilladrum and, dare I say… love.

> That is correct, sir. I believe our mutual friend and the young woodsman have fallen quite, quite in love.

> Indeed, I can see them both from my current perch on the sundial in the walled garden, sir (fear not, our mutual friend has lashed me down). And dashed if I'm not reminded of a ditty from my bear-hood, sir:

> Wren and Seamus sitting in a tree, K.I.S.S.I.N.G

Not a tree as such, sir. A tree house. And rather lovely it is, too. Which more or less brings me to my feeling, sir. A feeling that everything is going to work out very nicely for our mutual friend and the woodsman. Very nicey indeed.

As you were, sir. Enjoy your tea.

Your faithful servant, as always,

Herbert bear

Colin Collett put down his phone, dabbed his handkerchief gently at his right eye, then his left, *then* chuckled, *then* topped up his tea.

"Fly, my Wren," he said, smiling proudly, bringing his mug to his lips and raising it in a *Cheers* to the empty seat where his girl used to sit.

"Be happy, and just fly..."

The End

Also by Holly Wyld

♥ **Welcome to Primrose Island!** ♥

Titles in the Primrose Island novellas series:

A Scottish Island Surprise

One Spring at Tilladrum

A Girl Called Brodie

Lara's Lighthouse

The Island Castle

When Freya Met Magnus

♥ THE PRIMROSE ISLAND NOVELLAS ♥

✓ Heartwarming, standalone short stories

✓ Laugh-out-loud romantic comedy

✓ Wildly beautiful Scottish settings

✓ Characters to fall in love with

Perfect for fans of Scottish Highland romantic comedies from Jenny Colgan, Rachael Lucas, Lisa Hobman and Julie

Connect with Holly on Facebook!

www.facebook.com/authorhollywyld

Milton Keynes UK
Ingram Content Group UK Ltd.
UKHW010708290923
429627UK00005B/411